# EDDY B, PIGBOY

LIBRARY OF CONGRESS CATALOGING IN PUBLICATION DATA

Dunrea, Olivier. 1953-
Eddy B, pigboy.
"A Margaret K. McElderry book."
Summary: After a mama pig wanders off to have her
babies, it is Eddy B's job to find them and bring them
safely back to the pigsty on his father's farm.
[1. Pigs—Fiction.   2. Farm life—Fiction]
I. Title.
PZ7.D922Ed   1983   [E]        83-2832
ISBN 0-689-50277-X

Composition by Dix Type Inc., Syracuse, New York
Printed by Connecticut Printers
Bound by Halliday Lithograph Corporation

First Edition

# EDDY B, PIGBOY

*written and illustrated by*
**Olivier Dunrea**

*A Margaret K. McElderry Book*
ATHENEUM 1983 NEW YORK

For my mother and stepfather,
Marian and Ralph Getkin

My name is Eddy B.

I live on a farm.

I have a Pa, a Ma, two sisters, and a
little brother.

And a dog named Daisy D.

I work on my Pa's farm as a pigboy.

When a mama pig wanders off with
her babies, my job is to find them
because wild animals can hurt the
piglets.

So, I go out and hunt for the mama
pig. It's up to me to get her and her
babies home safe.

When I find the mama pig and the
piglets, I sneak up real quiet, and
quick as lightning grab one of the
piglets and hold on to it real tight.

Right away the little porker lets out
the loudest squeal you've ever heard.
That's when I start running back to
the farm as fast as I can.

When the mama pig hears her baby squealing like that, she wants to get whoever is hurting it. That's why she comes after me and that's why I run.

EEEEE E E

I head right for the pigsty running for
all I'm worth. Because if mama pig
catches me she can be awful mean and
bite hard. And mama pigs run fast.

As soon as I get to the pigsty I throw the little squealer in and, quick as I can, I jump onto the fence.

When I was little and not so fast, a mama pig tore out the seat of my pants as I was trying to climb the fence. I run real fast now.

Mama pig runs right into the sty to find her baby and all the other little ones follow right behind her as fast as they can. Pa shuts the gate real quick.

Mama pig makes sure her baby is okay.

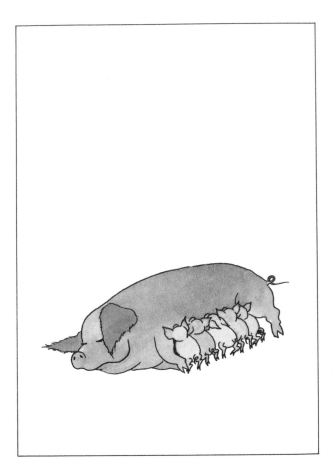

Then she lies down to nurse all of them.

My job is done.

For running as a pigboy Pa gives me a quarter. And with that quarter I buy the biggest ice cream soda in the world.

Then Daisy D and I go fishing.

And that's what a pigboy does.